Ana,
A Christmas ———
for your collection

May all your wishes
come true!
Love,
Mommy

On the Way to Christmas

by Tanya Shpakow

Alfred A. Knopf · New York

For my husband, Tom, with all my love

THIS IS A BORZOI BOOK
PUBLISHED BY ALFRED A. KNOPF, INC.

Copyright © 1991 by Tanya Shpakow
All rights reserved under International and Pan-American Copyright
Conventions. Published in the United States by Alfred A. Knopf, Inc.,
New York, and simultaneously in Canada by Random House of Canada
Limited, Toronto. Distributed by Random House, Inc., New York.

Library of Congress Cataloging-in-Publication Data
Shpakow, Tanya.
On the way to Christmas / by Tanya Shpakow.   p.   cm.
Summary: Relates the journey of a lost teddy bear as he makes his
way back to his little boy on the night before Christmas eve.
ISBN 0-679-81796-4 (trade)—ISBN 0-679-91796-9 (lib. bdg.)
[1. Teddy bears—Fiction. 2. Lost and found possessions—Fiction.
3. Christmas—Fiction.] I Title. PZ7.S5591440n 1991 [E]—dc20 90-5373

Manufactured in the United States of America
10 9 8 7 6 5 4 3 2 1
Book design by Edward Miller

The tag on Walter's wrist read PACK THIS TEDDY BEAR
INSIDE CAR. But the moving men didn't see it. The bear
was covered by a blanket and the tag was hidden. Walter
wondered why he wasn't with the little boy. He was riding
with the suitcases on top of the luggage rack.

The moving men had made a terrible mistake.

In the backseat the little boy woke from a restless sleep. Something was wrong.

"Stop the car!" he cried out. "We forgot Walter!" But Father couldn't stop. They had to reach the new house by Christmas.

"Try not to worry," Father said gently. "He must be in the moving van."

But what if Walter had been left behind?

Walter was miserable. Wind rocked the car, and snow made it hard to see. Each new gust tore at the blanket. Was the rope that held him coming loose? A suitcase moved beneath him!

A bump in the road was all it took....

The bear flew through the air. He watched the red taillights disappear into the snowstorm. Would the car come back for him?

Walter had almost given up when he heard a rumble. It sounded like a car engine. Headlights flashed. It must be the little boy's car!

The rumbling grew louder and LOUDER and LOUDER…

and a big, yellow snowplow roared around the corner!

Walter was scooped up and tossed into a great rolling pile of snow. Slush and ice chunks tumbled over him. The plow gave one final push and chugged away. The bear was left behind—upside down in a snowbank.

At sunrise, footsteps crunched nearby. Walter heard a
loud snort and the digging began. He could make out a
sweater. A hair ribbon brushed his face. This couldn't be
the little boy.

The bear was tugged free and carried away. His rescuer
barked, and a door flew open.

Walter was inside a beauty shop. The owner puzzled
over the tag attached to the ragged bear's wrist. Part of the
message was missing.

"Poor bear," she said, "you must be lost. We'll fix you
up and find you a home."

Walter was treated just like a customer. Then he was placed in the window with a sign that read HOMELESS BEAR—CLAIM ME. The dog slept beside him.

Many children passed the window. Walter was certain the little boy would find him now.

A woman stopped. She grinned—AT HIM!

"Don't look at *me*!" Walter panicked. He belonged to the little boy.

But the woman marched into the shop. "I know where *you* belong," she said as she reached for the bear.

The dog growled as she tore off the sign.

Walter left the shop in a cardboard box tied with a silk hair ribbon.

It was dark and stuffy inside the box. The bear was terribly confused. He wondered how the woman knew where he belonged. Did the little boy still miss him? Would the boy open the box when the right time came?

The box rocked. Walter banged his head hard. The ribbon snapped and someone lifted the lid.
Then came the loudest, highest shriek he ever heard.
   "*Yippppeeeeee!* I found one of my presents!"

The girl kicked the broken box aside and skipped back to her bedroom. In a singsong voice she chanted, "Mom thought she hid them ALL...but I'm *too-o-o* smart..."

Walter had never seen so many toys. Almost all of them looked broken. And now did he belong here, too?

The girl held her new present up to the light to get a better look. She pouted and stuck out her tongue.

"You're old and you smell funny," she screeched. "I don't want you!"

The girl giggled with delight as she tied some balloons
to Walter's leg. She unlatched the window and let him go.
''Good-bye, stupid bear,'' she called as he blew upward.

Colored lights twinkled below. Songs of carolers drifted
on the wind. It was Christmas Eve. The bear rose higher
and higher.

A light glimmered above him. But Walter wasn't
watching. He sighed and looked hopelessly at the
disappearing city. He knew he would never see the little
boy again.

Sleigh bells rang through the
sky. The light grew brighter.
''There you are,'' a big voice
boomed. ''I've been looking
for you!''

Walter was swept up and tucked into a warm red coat.

Then with a shout and a jingle off they flew...

to answer the Christmas wish of the little boy.